Job Wanted

by Teresa Bateman

illustrated by Chris Sheban

Holiday House / New York

For Eva, Evan, Blake and Brooklyn,
Cole and Cara, Emily, Landon, Jack
and Grace and Kaden—
welcome to the family!
T. B.

to Claire
C. S.

Library of Congress Cataloging-in-Publication Data
Bateman, Teresa.
Job wanted / by Teresa Bateman ; illustrated by Chris Sheban. — First edition.
pages cm
Summary: Arriving at a farm with sore paws and an empty stomach, a dog tries
to convince the farmer that he could be just as valuable as a cow, a horse,
or a chicken.
ISBN 978-0-8234-3391-9 (hardcover)
[1. Dogs—Fiction. 2. Farm life—Fiction. 3. Domestic animals—Fiction.]
I. Sheban, Chris, illustrator. II. Title.
PZ7.B294435Job 2015
[E]—dc23
2014039821

An old farm dog plodded down a dirt road—paws sore and stomach empty. When he reached a farm, he marched right up to the farmer.

"Do you need a dog?" he asked.

"No," the farmer replied. "Dogs just eat and don't give anything back. They're not like cows, or horses or chickens that pay for their keep."

"Do you have an opening for a cow?" the dog asked.

The farmer scratched his nose. "Well, sure. But you're not a cow."

"We'll see about that," the dog said. "I'll start work tomorrow."

The next morning the dog was up before dawn. He opened the barn door and herded the cows into place.

When the farmer saw all the cows ready and waiting, his eyes popped. He did the milking in jig time.

When he got to the last stall, the dog said, "*Moo.*"

The farmer shook his head. "I'll grant you it was handy having the cows ready, but you're not a cow, so I'm afraid there's no job for you here."

The dog was disappointed but not discouraged.

"Do you have an opening for a horse?" he asked.

The farmer scraped goo off his boots. "Well, sure. But you're not a horse."

"We'll see about that," the dog said. "I'll start work tomorrow."

When the farmer went to the barn early the next morning, the cows were all in their stalls ready to go.

"Hmmm," he said. The milking went quickly, leaving time to plow the field.

The farmer went out to hitch up the horse to the plow. Standing next to the horse was that dog again.

The dog said, "*Neigh.*"

The farmer frowned. "I appreciate your help with the cows, but this harness won't fit you."

He hooked up the plow and headed to the field. The horse trudged along at a snail's pace.

The dog hurried to the garden for a bunch of carrots. He ran in front of the horse, dangling the tasty orange treats just out of reach.

Soon the farmer was running behind the horse, hanging on to the plow for dear life. The plowing was done in jig time.

The farmer looked down at the dog. "You're still not a cow, and you're not a horse. There's no job for you here."

The dog was disappointed but not discouraged. "Do you have an opening for a chicken?" he asked.

The farmer fiddled with his straw hat. "Well, sure. But you're not a chicken."

"We'll see about that," the dog said. "I'll start work tomorrow."

The farmer went to put his feet up—something he'd never been able to do before.

The next morning the dog got the cows into the barn for milking, fed the horse some carrots then introduced himself to the hens.

The chicken coop was a mess, with dirty straw everywhere and the nest boxes all a-clutter.

"I'd better tidy it up," the dog declared.

So he cleaned out the whole thing and put fresh straw in all the nests. Soon the chickens were laying eggs in their boxes, clucking happily.

The dog built himself a cozy nest. Then he settled down for a nap before the farmer came to gather the eggs.

As he snoozed, a fox slipped slyly across the field. The farmer was in the barn milking the cows. The fox slid behind the stable and over to the chicken coop.

He reached in one furry paw to steal a chicken or an egg.

The floor was clean. He reached in farther, patting until he felt a big straw nest. His paw reached up and grabbed.

"*BARK-bark-bark-bark*," clucked the dog, scaring the fox so badly that he shot out of the barnyard and went running for the high hills.

The farmer heard the commotion and sprinted outside to see the fox—a streak of red heading south. He looked into the chicken coop.

The hens were all in their places and settling down again after the foofaraw. Everything was neat and tidy. Gathering eggs would be a breeze. Why, he could do it in jig time!

There in the middle was that dog. It was clear who he had to thank for there being any eggs, or chickens, at all.

The dog looked at him and said, "*Cluck.*"
The farmer hitched up his overalls.
"I'm sorry," he said. "I don't have any openings for cows. My horse position is filled. You're not quite right for chicken work. But I might have one job that just opened up."

The dog looked at the farmer and wagged his tail.
"I'm starting to think that what this farm needs
is a good dog," the farmer continued. "Do you think
you can handle the job?"

And the dog said, "*Ruff!*"